girl clothes

For my mother,
who I think would've been great
friends with Mary had they ever met.

Balzer + Bray is an imprint of HarperCollins Publishers.

Mary Wears What She Wants. Copyright © 2019 by Keith Negley.

The artist used aquarelle paper to create pencils and cut the illustrations for this book. Typography by Dana Fritts. Hand lettering by Aurora Parlagreco. 18 19 20 21 22 SCP 10 9 8 7 6 5 4 3 2 1 ❖ First Edition Originally inspired by the episode "Mary Walker Would Wear What She Wanted" from the podcast The Memory Palace.

Keith Negley

Mary Wears What She Wants

BALZER + BRAY
An Imprint of HarperCollinsPublishers

Once upon a time (but not too long ago), girls weren't allowed to wear pants.

Can you imagine?

The only thing girls could wear were uncomfortable dresses . . .

heavy-and-hot-and-hard-to-breathe-in dresses.

Tied-too-tight-and-can't-bend-over dresses!

It's the way things have always been and the way
things will always be, they said.
And no one thought it should be any different.

Actually, that last part's not entirely true. . . .
Mary thought it should be different, and
she had an idea.

A very daring idea.

A great idea!

Mary liked it so much she went into town to show everyone.

It was kind of a big deal.

And not everyone liked it.

"You're gonna regret wearing pants, Mary Walker!"
they all said.

"No, I won't!" Mary said back.

But she kind of did.

Mary didn't understand why everyone cared so much about
what she wore.

"They've never seen a girl wearing pants before," said her father.
"Sometimes people get scared of what they don't understand."

"So I should go back to wearing dresses?" asked Mary.
"I didn't say that," said her dad.

That night Mary didn't get a wink of sleep.

The next morning Mary decided she didn't like being told what to wear. Pants were just plain better in all sorts of ways.

As she left for school, she discovered she could even walk faster in pants . . .

which Mary really appreciated.

But when Mary got to school it was more of the same. She started to worry this was how things were going to be from now on.

"I'd like to go to school, please," said Mary.
"But you're wearing boys' clothes!" they all said.

"I'm not wearing boys' clothes," said Mary. "I'm wearing *my* clothes! Now, if you'll excuse me, please, I'm late for school."

And with that she pushed through the door and went inside, prepared for even more of the same.

Except . . . it wasn't the same at all!

And it was never the same again.

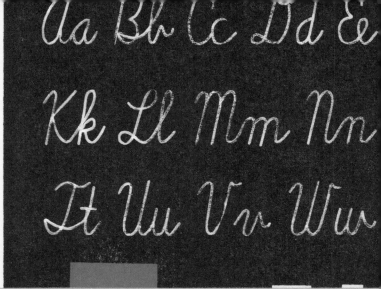

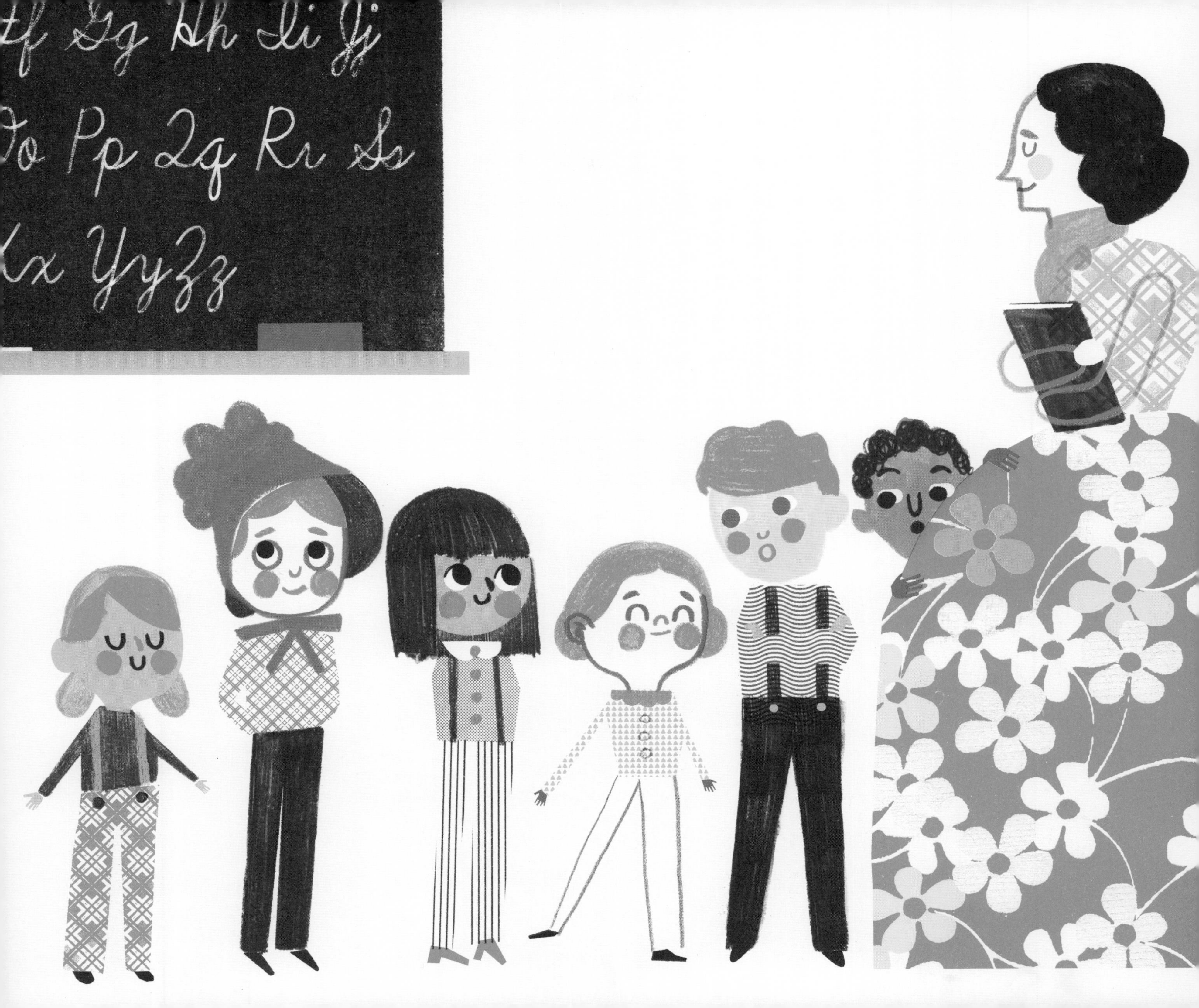
Gg Hh Ii Jj
Pp Qq Rr Ss
Yy Zz

Mary Edwards Walker was born in 1832 in Oswego, New York. She developed a keen sense of independence and a zeal for justice early on in her life that was far ahead of her time. She was one of the first women known to wear pants, which must've been a shocking notion. As she grew older, she was arrested repeatedly for it, for which she said in her defense: "I don't wear men's clothes, I wear my own clothes."

She went on to graduate from medical school in 1855 at a time when many people said women shouldn't. She volunteered with the Union Army in 1861 and was a surgeon in the Civil War, even though many people believed women couldn't. She often worked behind enemy lines and was eventually captured by Confederates. They demanded that she wear a dress, but no matter how hard they tried, she wouldn't.

In 1865, Dr. Mary Walker was awarded the Congressional Medal of Honor, the highest military decoration that can be given. She was very proud and wore it every day, and as of the time that this book was written, she is the only woman to have received it.

Mary spent the rest of her life writing, lecturing, and fighting for women's rights to vote and to wear what they want. Mary continued to wear what she wanted (and cause a stir) until her death in 1919 at the ripe age of eighty-seven.

We can thank Mary Walker the teacher, surgeon, war hero, writer, and activist for challenging the social norms of her day and paving the way for us so that we can all enjoy the right to wear what we want.

boy clothes